William Taylor Adams

Uncle Ben

A Story for Little Folks

William Taylor Adams

Uncle Ben
A Story for Little Folks

ISBN/EAN: 9783743373235

Manufactured in Europe, USA, Canada, Australia, Japa

Cover: Foto ©Andreas Hilbeck / pixelio.de

Manufactured and distributed by brebook publishing software
(www.brebook.com)

William Taylor Adams

Uncle Ben

The Riverdale Books.

———∞⚬∞———

UNCLE BEN.

A STORY FOR LITTLE FOLKS.

BY

OLIVER OPTIC,

AUTHOR OF "THE BOAT CLUB," "ALL ABOARD," "NOW OR NEVER," "TRY
AGAIN," "POOR AND PROUD," "LITTLE BY LITTLE," &c.

BOSTON:
LEE AND SHEPARD,
(SUCCESSORS TO PHILLIPS, SAMPSON & CO.)
1866.

·

ELECTROTYPED AT THE
BOSTON STEREOTYPE FOUNDRY.

UNCLE BEN.

I.

FRANK and Flora Lee, with Charley Green and his two sisters, Katy and Nellie, had gone out to spend the afternoon in the pasture. It was July, and the strawberries in the fields were ripe. The children had brought their tin pails with them, and they hoped to be able to fill them with berries before they went home.

The afternoon was quite warm, and they soon got tired of running after strawberries, for there were very few in the field. Seating themselves under the broad branches of an oak, they rested their weary limbs, cooled their heated blood, and ate up the few berries that they had picked.

The pasture was on the outskirts of the village, and next to the river. On one side of it was an old, unpainted house, in which lived a man by the name of Benjamin Gorham. He was a poor man, but he was as proud as he was poor. He had been a sailor nearly all his lifetime. He was too old to go to sea now, and had come to Riverdale to end his days in peace and quiet.

He had bought the old house in which he lived, together with the few acres of land around it. He had very little money, and the people of Riverdale thought he must have a hard time to get along. He worked on the land, and raised fruits and vegetables, which he sold in the village.

It seemed very sad for an

old man like him to work so
hard for a living. The town,
or the people, of Riverdale
would very gladly have helped
him with money or provisions,
but he was too proud to take
any thing from them. People
pitied him, and wanted to do
something for him; but he was
angry when any one offered
to give him any thing.

The folks in Riverdale had
a habit of calling Mr. Gorham

Uncle Ben, though for what reason I am unable to say; for not many of them liked him very well, and when any of the children came upon his land, he drove them away. He was cross, and scolded a great deal more than was necessary.

But the world had used him rather badly, judging from his own talk. He had worked hard all his life, and now, when

he was an old man, he had
not enough to live upon without severe toil. I suppose this
was what made him cross.
He thought people pitied him,
and he did not want to be
pitied, because he was very
proud.

Uncle Ben had not always
been a common sailor while
at sea. He had been the first
mate of a ship — which is next
to the captain — the two last

voyages he had made. He had wanted to be a captain, but the owners, for some reason or other, would not trust him.

This made him gloomy and sad. He was disappointed, and this helped to make him cross. People used to vex and bother him, too, because he was so crusty, and this only made him worse. His wife was a very good woman, and all the neighbors liked her very much. They had no children.

The happy party were seated only a little way from the house of Uncle Ben ; but the two boys thought they were as near as they wanted to be, for the old man seemed to hate children.

If he did, it was only because they gave him so much trouble. They knew he was cross, and they liked to plague him. On purpose to bother him, they used to steal his apples, even when they had enough of them. They would get into his lot, or his garden, only to see him run after them.

This was very naughty of them, for I have no doubt, if they had been kind to him, he would have been kind to them.

"I wish I had a drink of water," said Flora Lee, as she

glanced at the house of Uncle Ben. "I'm almost choked."

"We can get some at the spring," said Frank.

"Yes, but the spring is clear out at the other end of the pasture," added Charley.

"Why can't we get some water at Uncle Ben's?" asked Flora.

"He wouldn't let you step on his land. He is a cross old fellow."

"Why, he would let me have some water. Of course he would," added Flora.

"No, he wouldn't; he drives the fellows off when they come near his house," said Charley Green.

" I'm almost sure, if I should ask him, he would give me some water."

"No, he wouldn't; he would drive you off, just as he has hundreds of others. There he is now, in the garden, picking his currants," replied Charley, pointing to the place where the currant bushes lined the fence.

"I heard my father say the boys plague him almost to death; and that must be the reason why he is so cross."

"That may be, but he is as cross as he can be, whatever the reason is."

"Poor old man! It is too

bad for the boys to plague him.
They say he has been all over
the world, and sailed upon all
the oceans."

"I know he has," added
Charley. "He told my father
something about one of his
voyages. Father says he likes
to tell stories when he can get
any one to hear him."

"I should like to hear him,"
said Flora; "I could sit all
the afternoon and listen to

stories about the sea; about sailors and such things."

"So could I."

"I am going down to his house to get a drink of water," continued Flora.

"I wouldn't go there," said Frank.

"I am not afraid of him," replied the brave little girl. "I will be kind to him, and I know he won't hurt me. I don't believe he will even scold at me. If he does I can go away, you know."

"Better go to the spring."

"Besides, when I get down there, I mean to ask him to tell us a story."

"He will bite your head off if you do," said Katy Green.

"I don't believe he will; at any rate, I shall try him. If you don't want to go, you may stay where you are."

"I will go, too," said Nellie.

The children talked it over a little while, and they concluded that Flora and Nellie should go alone, and that the others should wait in the road for them.

So they went down the hill into the road, and the three who were to wait seated themselves under a tree near the house. The two little girls walked on, and entered the yard in front of the house.

Uncle Ben was picking currants, not far off, and they made their way to the spot, being very careful not to tread upon any of the plants.

As they came near to the old man, he heard their steps, and turned to see who they were. He looked very sour and cross, and Flora began to have some doubts in regard to her mission, which was not only to get some water, but to see if Uncle Ben would not speak kindly to her. He did not look as if he could speak a pleasant word, even if he tried ever so hard.

"What do you want here?" growled the old man, in a tone that made the little girls tremble with fear.

"Please, sir, I am very dry. Will you please to let me have a drink of water?"

"There is the well; you can

help yourself," replied Uncle
Ben, in much gentler tones
than before.

"Thank you, sir; we won't
tread on any thing, nor do a
bit of harm."

Flora thought Uncle Ben
was trying to smile as she
turned to go; but she was cer-
tain he did not smile. For my
part I don't see how he could
help smiling, when he looked
upon such a good girl as Flora.

Uncle Ben assists the Girls.

II.

WHEN Flora and Nellie arrived at the well, there was no water in the bucket. It was drawn with a long pole, called a " sweep," supported on a crotched post. The bucket was attached to a small pole, fastened to the end of the long one, which went down into the well.

As the bucket went down, one end of the long pole came down with it, while the other end went up — just as the beam does in a pair of scales. It was hard work to draw water with a sweep, and the little girls found that the strength of both of them was not enough to move it.

While they were trying, they saw Uncle Ben leave his work, and walk over to the well.

They wondered what he was coming for, as they could not believe that one so cross as people said he was would think of helping them.

"That is rather too hard work for such little girls," said he, as he pulled down the sweep, and then drew up the bucket full of water.

"Thank you, sir," said Flora. "You are so kind!"

"What is your name, my

little girl?" asked Uncle Ben, pleasantly.

"Flora Lee, sir; and this is Nellie Green."

"You have been in the pasture—haven't you?"

"Yes, sir; we have been trying to find some strawberries, but they were so scarce we couldn't get many," replied Flora, when she had taken a good drink of the pure cold water.

"There were more of you, I thought."

"Yes, sir; my brother and Nellie's brother and sister are waiting for us out there in the road."

"I will tell you where you can find plenty of strawberries," said Uncle Ben; and now, without a doubt, there was a smile on his wrinkled face.

"O, thank you, sir!" exclaimed Flora, with childlike pleasure.

"In my pasture, on the other side of the road, there are oceans of them."

"But will you let us pick them, sir?"

"You may; when that Joe Birch and such boys as he come round here, I always send them off, because they steal my fruit, and break down my fences. They are very bad boys," replied Uncle Ben, who seemed to feel the need of telling them why he was so cross.

"Uncle" — Flora was going to say "Uncle Ben;" but she did not know that it would be quite proper for her to call him by this name.

"That's right, little lady; call me 'Uncle Ben.' You needn't be at all afraid of me. That's just what the sailors used to call me on board ship."

"That's just what I was going to say, Uncle Ben. People say you have been all over the world."

"I have, almost."

"We should dearly like to have you tell us some stories about the sea, and places where you have been."

"I will do so, with pleasure," answered the old man,

with a smile — and so pleasant a smile that Flora and Nellie could hardly believe he was the man whom folks talked about so badly.

"Thank you. How kind you are! Will you tell us one now?"

"I can't very well, now. I have half a bushel of currants to pick before sundown."

"O, we will all help you, Uncle Ben, if you will only

tell us a sea story — won't we, Nellie ? "

" Yes, we will; there are five of us, and we can pick them as fast as any thing."

" Just as you please, little misses."

" We will go and call Frank, and Charley, and Katy," shouted Flora, as she ran out of the yard, followed by Nellie.

They were much pleased with the success of their mission. They felt as smart as though they had conquered a wild tiger. They were sure now that Uncle Ben did not hate children, as people said he did.

The old man had his faults, and they were serious faults too; but he was not half so bad as folks said he was. He was cross, very cross, at times, and this made others impose upon him. When he saw that

people were against him, without stopping to ask the reason, he began to hate them.

Things of this kind almost
always go on from bad to
worse ; and the more folks
" picked upon him," the more
he hated them. The boys,
and even the girls, who lived
near him, used to insult him,
when they dared to do so.
All these things put together
made him very unhappy.

The children under the tree jumped up when they saw Flora and Nellie running towards them so fast; and they at once concluded that Uncle Ben must have driven them out of his yard.

"I knew he would," said Charley.

"So did I," added Katy; "and they were fools to go near him."

"So you have come, at

last?" continued Charley, as the two little girls reached the tree.

"Yes; and got driven away, as I knew you would," said Katy.

"No, we didn't get driven away," puffed Flora, out of breath with running.

"Didn't he send you off?" asked Frank.

"Indeed he did not," answered Flora. "I don't care

what any body says about Uncle Ben; I say he is a real nice man—isn't he, Nellie?"

"Yes, he is."

"He is enough sight better than some of the folks that talk about him. I like him ever so much—don't you, Nellie?"

"Yes, indeed I do!"

"Tell us all about it," said Charley. "Did he scold at

you any?　Wasn't he cross and ugly?"

"He spoke cross when we first went to him; but after I asked him if I might have some water, he was just as good as pie," replied Flora.

"What did you say to him?"

"I only asked him if he would please to let me have some water.　He said I might; and when we couldn't draw the water ourselves, he came and drew it for us."

"Uncle Ben did?" exclaimed Charley.

"Yes, indeed he did," replied Nellie.

"Well, I shall give up now! Only think of Uncle Ben drawing a bucket of water for you!" said Frank.

"Why shouldn't he?" asked Flora.

"He should, but I don't believe he will get over it for a month. He will certainly have a fit after it."

"No, he won't," said Flora, smartly. "And I haven't told you the whole yet."

"What else? Wonders will never cease after this," laughed Frank.

"When I had taken a good drink of the water, I asked Uncle Ben if he wouldn't tell us a story."

" And he told you he would ? "

" He did."

"That will be first rate!" exclaimed Katy; "I do like to hear stories."

" When will he tell us one ? "

" I asked him if he wouldn't tell us one now. And he said, he would, only he had to pick half a bushel of currants before sundown. What do you think I told him then ? "

"I don't know; what did you tell him?" asked Charley.

"I told him we would all help him. You will — won't you?"

They all, even Katy, who was not often willing to do what her friends asked her to do, declared that they would.

They were so pleased at the idea of a story from Uncle Ben, that they were willing to buy the pleasure by picking his currants for him. Flora led the way back to the old man's house. He met them with a smile on his face, and led them out to the bushes, where they went to work.

It turned out that Uncle Ben had picked more than half the currants he wanted himself, and in less than half an hour the busy fingers of the children had finished the job.

Uncle Ben then led them to an apple tree near the house. Seating himself on the ground, the children gathered around him, and he began the story. The little folks could scarcely believe that he was the cross old man, whom almost every body hated, for he looked as good natured as any body could look.

On the Cross-trees.

III.

I HAVE no doubt my little readers will wish they were members of the party under the apple tree, hearing the story which the Riverdale children enjoyed so much, and which produced a lasting impression on their minds; and for their benefit I will repeat it.

UNCLE BEN'S STORY.

"When I was a young man, I went out on a whaling voyage. I suppose you don't know much about whaling; so I will tell you. The oil which you burn in your lamps is the fat of the whale. It is 'tried out,' just as they do hog's fat.

"A whale is a great big fish; some of them are a good deal longer than my barn there. Ships that go out to catch whales are often three or four years away from home, and go off thousands of miles.

"The ship has a great many boats, which are hoisted up at the sides. The men go out in the boats, and when they catch a whale, tow it to the ship.

"Almost up at the top of the mast, and more than a hundred feet from the water, there are two sticks, which are called the cross-trees. When the ship reaches any part of the ocean where whales are found, men are sent up to the cross-trees to look out.

" When a whale is seen, one of the men calls out, 'There she blows!' This great fish draws water into his mouth, and then blows it up in the air; and this is what they mean by 'blowing.'

" When the men on deck hear this cry, they find out where the whale is, and then get out the boats and go after him. They row up to the huge monster of the deep with very little noise, and then throw one or two harpoons into. him.

" A harpoon is a kind of iron spear, with a wooden handle, to which a long rope is fastened. When the whale feels the iron, he dives down into the deep, or runs away as fast as he can. Sometimes he drags the boat after him at a frightful speed, for many miles ; and it often happens that the men in the boat have to cut the line, in order to saves their lives.

"When the whale is weak from loss of blood, and tired out, the boat again steals upon him, and a long lance is thrust into his body. This kills him, if it is well done.

"Very often, when the men attack the whale, he turns upon the boat, and breaks it all to pieces with a single slap of his tail, or crushes it all to bits in his monstrous mouth. The sailors always have a hard time, and are often killed, in their efforts to conquer the whale.

"When they get the whale

alongside the ship, they cut out the fat, or 'blubber,' in long strips, and hoist it on board the vessel. It is then chopped up in small pieces, and tried out in great kettles. The oil is put in barrels, and stowed in the hold.

"I have told you how to catch a whale, so that you may understand the story which I am now going to tell you.

"I sailed in the ship Jane, for the South Pacific Ocean, long before any of you were born; and I guess it was before either of your fathers was born. We went round Cape Horn, which is a very stormy place, and came near being cast away in a heavy gale.

"But when we got into the Pacific Ocean we had fine weather, and at last reached the 'feeding ground.' Though

the whale is a monstrous crea-
ture, he feeds upon animals
called 'squid,' and small fishes.
Of course he must live where
he can find his food.

"One day I was up on the
cross-trees, looking out on the
ocean for whales. I had with
me a boy of about twelve
years of age. He was as pretty a boy as ever I saw. He
had fair, brown hair, which
curled in beautiful ringlets on

his cheeks and neck, just as Miss Flora's does, only it was not so long.

"We all loved that boy, for he was a brave and noble little fellow. He was gentle and kind to the men, and always obeyed the orders of the officers at once. He was our pet, and we all treated him just like a younger brother.

"He could read well, and wrote a handsome hand, and

when he first came on board
the ship, I knew he couldn't be
the son of very poor parents,
for he did not speak like boys
brought up in the street, and
his hand was as white and
soft as that of a fine lady.

"One day I was up on the
cross-trees, and George was
with me, as I said before.
We were on the lookout for
whales, and he was just as
anxious to discover one as

though he had been the captain of the ship. He had no
hat on then, and his pretty
brown locks blew out in the
wind, just like Miss Flora's
here.

"Says I, 'George, why did
you come to sea?'

"'Because I wanted to, of
course,' replied he. 'What
makes you ask that question?'

"'Does your mother know
where you are, George?'

"He looked sad when I spoke of his mother. I knew very well he must have run away from home, for a boy with such nice white hands as he had when he came aboard the ship, had no need to go to sea. He had never been brought up to work, but he never grumbled once at his duty, or the coarse food of the sailor.

"'Ah, George,' I said, 'I

am afraid you ran away from your mother.'

"'I did, Ben.'

"'Haven't you sent her a letter, so that she may know where you are?'

"'No; I would not have her know I am aboard a whale ship for all the world,' said he; and I was sure by the sad look on his face that he was sorry for what he had done.

" 'But you must write to her, George, the very first chance you get.'

" 'I can't do that, Ben. It would kill her to know where I am. I have heard her say a great many times that she had rather lay me in the grave than have me go to sea in a whale ship.'

" 'But only think of her living for two or three years without knowing where you are! No doubt she wets her pillow with tears every night as she thinks of you. No, George; you must write to her, and let her know that you are alive and well. You can say in the letter that you are in a good ship, among good friends, and promise her that you will be a good boy. Perhaps she will feel easier then.'

" ' I can't write to her, Ben.'

" 'But you must, my boy. If you don't, I shall write to her by the first return ship I can find.'

" 'Please don't; she will feel a great deal worse if you write.'

" 'I will not, if you will promise to write yourself.'

" 'I will, then. I don't like to, though.'

" I could not bear the idea of having the little fellow's

mother pining over him for years, and I knew she would feel better to know he was alive, even if he was in a whale ship.

"Pretty soon after we had this talk, I saw a whale far off on the sea. In a few minutes we had a boat out, and George and I were pulling away towards the great fish. —There comes Mr. Jones for the currants, and I will tell

you the rest of the story as
soon as I have put them in
his wagon."

The dying Sailor Boy.

IV.

UNCLE Ben was absent but a few moments; yet it seemed like a long while to the children, who were very anxious to hear the rest of the story about the handsome sailor boy.

"Let me see—where did I leave off?" said Uncle Ben, as he again took his seat.

"You were just going away in the boat after the whale," replied Flora.

"So I was. Well, we rowed close up to the whale, and sent one iron into him. Before we could strike him again, he turned upon us, and with one blow smashed our frail boat all to pieces."

"Dear me!" exclaimed little Flora, with a shudder.

"Another boat from the ship

picked us up. George was a good swimmer, but I saw that he was sinking this time, and I bore him up in my arms, till he was taken into the boat. I found that he was badly hurt, for his face was deadly pale, and he was so faint he could hardly speak. We had lost the whale; so we went back to the ship.

"I carried George in my arms to the deck, and then

bore him to his bunk in the forecastle.

"That was a room to sleep in — wasn't it?" asked Nellie.

"Yes, child, but it wasn't any such place as your chamber. It was cold, dark, and damp. I laid the poor boy in his bunk, and tried to find out where he was hurt; but he was so weak he could tell me nothing.

"If he had been my own son, I could not have felt any worse. I could not help thinking of his poor mother, as I sat by the side of his bunk, watching over him. What would she have said if she could see her darling child, sick in that dirty, dark place? How she would have wept!

"I did not think poor George was very badly hurt; I did not want to think so, and I suppose this is the reason why I did not. The captain went down to see him, and then got some medicine for him.

"In the evening he seemed to be a little better, and I hoped he would be well in a day or two. He talked a little with me, and told me where his pains were. He spoke of his mother and his home, and seemed to feel very sad to be so far away from them.

"I sat by his side till eight bells — that is, till twelve o'-clock. He slept much of the time, and as I bent over him and listened to his quiet breathing, I thought he was better, and that he would be able to go on deck the next day.

"You don't know much about the life of a whaler, I suppose; so you can't tell how tired and worn out he gets sometimes. The boats are of-

ten out all night, and the men
have to row, when they are so
sleepy and tired that they can
hardly hold their heads up.

"Well, I had been out in the
boat all the night before, and
I was just as tired as a man
could be. I could hardly keep
my eyes open, as I sat at the
side of the poor sick boy; but
I did not once lose myself
while I was on this duty.

"At twelve o'clock, finding

that George slept easily, I called one of my shipmates to take my place. He was very willing to do so; but before I left him, I charged him, over and over again, to keep awake and mind the boy. He promised me he would, and I went to my bunk.

"I was so tired that I slept like a rock till eight bells, which was four o'clock in the morning. My first thought was of poor George, and jumping out of my berth, I hastened to his side. My shipmate whom I had left to watch him was fast asleep.

"I felt so very angry with him, that only my desire to learn how the sick boy was, prevented me from kicking him out of the forecastle. I looked into the bunk, and all was still as when I had left, and I thought he was asleep.

" All was still and calm in the berth — so still and calm that I trembled with fear. I listened to hear his breathing, but no sound reached my ear. I then placed my hand upon his brow. It was as cold as marble.

" Poor George was dead!

" O children, I can't tell you how I felt then. It seemed just as though our angel had been taken out of the ship.

I wept as I should have wept
if he had been my son or my
brother.

"From that sleep in which
I had left him he had never
awakened, for he lay just as
he was at midnight. There
was not a dry eye in the ship
when it was told that poor
George, whom we all loved,
was dead.

"We dressed him in his
clean clothes, and bore his

body upon deck, where we covered it with the American flag. At noon the sad cry of ' All hands to bury the dead' sounded gloomily through the ship.

" The body of poor George, sewed up in a piece of sail-cloth, was placed on a plank, still covered with the American flag. It was raised upon the rail, ready to be cast into the sea.

"The captain, with his eyes brim full of tears, and hardly able to speak from grief, read prayers; and all was ready to launch the body into the deep. The canvas had been left open at the head, and the wind blew the fair brown locks upon the cold brow of poor George, just as when he had stood by my side on the cross-trees.

"One by one the sailors kissed his marble cheeks, —

kissed him for his mother,—
and wiped the tears from their
brown faces. The canvas was
sewed up, the word was given,
and the body slid off the plank
into the great ocean, there to
sleep till the graves give up
their dead.

"The ship filled away upon
her course, and it was many
and many a day before we
ceased to think of the poor
sailor boy in his ocean grave.

"When I got home, I went to New York to see poor George's mother. I found her without trouble, and told her the story of her lost child. A few days after she was taken to an insane asylum, where she died. Poor George! Poor mother!"

Every one of the children was crying when Uncle Ben finished his story, and even when they went home, their eyes were red and swollen with weeping.

"What is the matter, Flora?" asked Mrs. Lee, when her two children entered the house.

"Nothing, mother."

"Why, both of you have been crying! What has happened?"

"Nothing, mother; only Uncle Ben has been telling us a very sad story about a handsome sailor boy, who was killed at sea by a whale," replied Frank.

"Who told you the story — Uncle Ben?" asked Mrs. Lee, very much surprised.

"Yes, mother," replied Flora. "He is a real nice man, and not a bit cross when you don't bother him."

The children told their father and mother all about the events of the afternoon, and how kind Uncle Ben had been to them. Mr. Lee was very much pleased, as well as surprised, for he looked upon Uncle Ben just as nearly all the people of Riverdale did — as a hard and cross man.

But after what the children had told him, he felt very kindly towards the old man, and wanted to do something for him, so that he need not have to work so hard. He went to see Uncle Ben the next day, and told him how pleased the children had been with him.

A few months after this event Mr. Lee, with the help of his friends, got the place of Postmaster of Riverdale for Uncle Ben, and the old man sold his farm and moved into the village. This place gave him money enough to live without hard work. He had got it by being kind to the children, and after this he tried very hard to be kind to every body.

So you see how much good Flora did by going to Uncle Ben in the right way. She had conquered his cold heart, and the old man, feeling how much he owed to the children, became a great favorite among them.

Many a time, after Uncle

Ben had sent off the mail, the children gathered together in the Post Office, to hear an interesting story of the sea; and even the old folks were glad to listen to them.

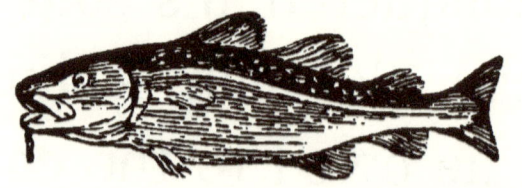

www.ingramcontent.com/pod-product-compliance
Lightning Source LLC
Chambersburg PA
CBHW020040030726
47499CB00007B/2508